Hoddley Poddley

Favourite Rhymes and Verse

chosen by
Margaret Mayo

ORCHARD BOOKS

For Anna and Jack

ORCHARD BOOKS
96 Leonard Street, London EC2A 4XD
Orchard Books Australia
Unit 31/56 O'Riordan Street, Alexandria, NSW 2015
ISBN 1 84121 697 6
First published in Great Britain in 2001
Text compilation © Margaret Mayo 2001
The illustrator acknowledgements on pages 4 - 7
constitute an extension of this copyright page.
Illustrations © of the individual illustrators credited, 2001
The moral rights of Margaret Mayo and the
illustrators have been asserted in accordance with
the Copyright, Designs and Patents Act, 1988.
A CIP catalogue record for this book is available from the British Library.
10 9 8 7 6 5 4 3 2 1
Printed in Hong Kong/China

Contents

What a Nose!

The elephant goes like this, like that.

He's terrible big.

He's terrible fat.

He has no fingers,

And he has no toes,

But goodness gracious,

What a nose!

Animal Fair

I went to the animal fair.
The birds and the beasts were there.
   By the light of the moon,
   The giddy baboon
Was combing his auburn hair.
The monkey gave a jump—
Right onto the elephant's trunk.
   The elephant sneezed
   And fell on his knees,
So what became of the monkey, monkey,
Monkey, monkey, monk . . .

(Say all over again, getting faster and faster!)

The Yak

Yickity-yackity, yickity-yak,
the yak has a scriffily, scraffily back;
some yaks are brown yaks and some yaks are black,
yickity-yackity, yickity-yak.

Sniggildy-snaggildy, sniggildy-snag,
the yak is all covered with shiggildy-shag;
he walks with a ziggildy-zaggildy-zag,
sniggildy-snaggildy, sniggildy-snag.

Yickity-yackity, yickity-yak,
the yak has a scriffily, scraffily back;
some yaks are brown yaks and some yaks are black,
yickity-yackity, yickity-yak.

Jack Prelutsky

11

I Beg Your Pardon

What do you suppose?
A bee sat on my nose.
Then what do you think?
He gave me a wink
And said, "I beg your pardon,
I thought you were the garden."

This little pig had a scrub-a-dub-dub,
This little pig had a rub-a-dub-dub,
This little pig ran upstairs,
This little pig called out, "BEARS!"
Down came a jar with a loud
        SLAM! SLAM!
And this little pig ate all the jam.

Humpty Dumpty sat on a wall,
Eating ripe bananas.
Where do you think he put the skins?
Down the king's pyjamas!

Mary had a little lamb,
He had a sooty foot,
And into Mary's bread and jam
His sooty foot he put!

Baa, baa, black sheep
Have you any spots?
Yes, sir, yes, sir,
I've got lots.
Some on my tummy,
Some on my toes,
And one very big one
On the end of my nose.

Hopaloo Kangaroo

If you can jigaloo
jigaloo
I can do
the jigaloo too
for I'm the jiggiest
jigaloo kangaroo

If you can boogaloo
boogaloo
I can do
the boogaloo too
for I'm the boogiest
boogaloo kangaroo

But bet you can't hopaloo
hopaloo
like I can do
for I'm the hoppiest
hopaloo kangaroo

Gonna show you steps
you never knew.
And guess what, guys?
My baby in my pouch
will be dancing too.

John Agard (extract)

American jump, American jump,
One . . . two . . . three!
Over the land, under the sea,
Round the world and home for tea.

Down the
slippery slide
they slid,
Sitting slightly sideways;
Slipping . . .
sliding . . .
see them skid,
On holidays and Fridays.

The Jumblies

Far and few, far and few,
Are the lands where the Jumblies live;
Their heads are green, and their hands are blue,
And they went to sea in a sieve.

They sailed to the Western Sea, they did,
To a land all covered with trees,
And they bought an owl,
And a useful cart,
And a pound of rice, and a cranberry tart,
And a hive of silvery bees.

And they bought a pig,
And some green jackdaws,
And a lovely monkey with lollipop paws,
And forty bottles of Ring-Bo-Ree,
And no end of Stilton cheese.

Far and few, far and few
Are the lands where the Jumblies live;
Their heads are green, and their hands are blue,
And they went to sea in a sieve.

Edward Lear (extract)

There Was a Little Girl

There was a little girl who had a little curl
Right in the middle of her forehead;
When she was good she was very, very good,
But when she was bad she was horrid.

Little Arabella Miller
Found a furry caterpillar.
First it crawled upon her mother,
Then upon her baby brother.
Both cried, "Arabella Miller,
Take away that caterpillar!"

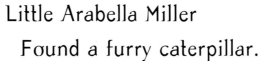

18

The Princess Priscilla

When the Princess Priscilla goes out
There aren't *any* dragons about;
   The dragons decide
   It is better to hide
While the Princess Priscilla is out.

As the Princess Priscilla goes by
There's a kind of a gleam in her eye –
   The tail of no dragon
   Could possibly wag on
When the Princess Priscilla goes by.

E. V. Rieu

The Frog on the Log

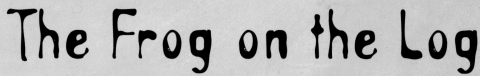

There once
Was a green
    Little **frog, frog, frog** –

Who played
In the wood
    On a **log, log, log!**

A screech owl
Sitting
    In a **tree, tree, tree** –

Came after
The frog
    With a **scree, scree, scree!**

When the frog
Heard the owl
    In a **flash, flash, flash** –

He leaped
In the pond
    With a **splash, splash, splash!**

Ilo Orleans

High in the pine tree
The little turtle dove
Made a nursery
To please her little love.
"*Coo!*" said the turtle dove.
"*Coo!*" said she,
In the long shady branches
Of the dark pine tree.

In Summer, when the days are hot,
Cat likes to find a shady spot,
And hardly move a single bit –
And sit –
and sit –
and sit –
and sit!

The Wheels on the Bus

The wheels on the bus go
Round and round,
Round and round,
Round and round.
The wheels on the bus go
Round and round,
All day long.

The driver on the bus says, **"Move along, please!**
Move along, please! Move along, please!"
The driver on the bus says, **"Move along, please!"**
All day long.

The horn on the bus goes **beep-beep-beep!**
Beep-beep-beep! Beep-beep-beep!
The horn on the bus goes **beep-beep-beep!**
All day long.

The wipers on the bus go **swish-swish-swish,**
Swish-swish-swish, swish-swish-swish,
The wipers on the bus go **swish-swish-swish,**
All day long.

The people on the bus go **bumpety-bump,**
Bumpety-bump, bumpety-bump.
The people on the bus go **bumpety-bump,**
All day long.

The children on the bus go **chatter chatter chatter,**
Chatter chatter chatter, chatter chatter chatter.
The children on the bus go **chatter chatter chatter,**
All day long.

The babies on the bus go **wah-wah-wah!**
Wah-wah-wah! Wah-wah-wah!
The babies on the bus go **wah-wah-wah!**
All day long.

The mums and dads on the bus go
Sshh-sshh-sshh!
Sshh-sshh-sshh! Sshh-sshh-sshh!
The mums and dads on the bus go
Sshh-sshh-sshh!
All day long.

ClicK Whirr Whisity ClicK

Tick-a-tock-a, tick!

Slowly ticks the big clock;
Tick-tock, tick-tock!
But cuckoo clock ticks double-quick;
Tick-a-tock-a, tick-a-tock-a,
Tick-a-tock-a, tick!

Our Washing Machine

Our washing machine went whisity whirr
Whisity whisity whisity whirr
One day at noon it went whisity click
Whisity whisity whisity click
Click grr click grr click grr click
Call the repairman
Fix it . . . Quick!

Patricia Hubbell

Engineers

Pistons, valves and wheels and gears
That's the life of engineers
Thumping, chunking engines going
Hissing steam and whistles blowing.

There's not a place I'd rather be
Than working round machinery
Listening to that clanking sound
Watching all the wheels go round.

Jimmy Garthwaite

The Sleeping Princess

There was a princess long ago,
Long ago, long ago;
There was a princess long ago,
Long long ago.

An ancient castle was her home,
Was her home, was her home;
An ancient castle was her home,
Long long ago.

But a wicked fairy cast a spell,
Cast a spell, cast a spell;
But a wicked fairy cast a spell,
Long long ago.

The princess climbed a big high tower,
A big high tower, a big high tower;
The princess climbed a big high tower,
Long long ago.

There she pricked her little thumb,
Her little thumb, her little thumb;
There she pricked her little thumb,
Long long ago.

The princess slept a hundred years,
A hundred years, a hundred years;
The princess slept a hundred years,
Long long ago.

A great thick hedge grew giant high,
Giant high, giant high;
A great thick hedge grew giant high,
Long long ago.

A handsome prince came galloping by,
Galloping by, galloping by;
A handsome prince came galloping by,
Long long ago.

He cut the hedge down with his sword,
With his sword, with his sword;
He cut the hedge down with his sword,
Long long ago.

He took her hand and kissed her once,
Kissed her once, kissed her once;
He took her hand and kissed her once,
Long long ago.

She woke up and married him,
Married him, married him;
She woke up and married him,
Long long ago.

Everyone was happy then,
Happy then, happy then;
Everyone was happy then,
Long long ago.

OINK! BAA! CLUCK! QUACK! MOO!

I went to visit a farm one day
And saw a pig across the way.
Now what do you think I heard it say?
OINK!
  OINK!
    OINK!

I went to visit a farm one day
And saw a sheep across the way.
Now what do you think I heard it say?
BAA!
  BAA!
    BAA!

I went to visit a farm one day
And saw a hen across the way.
Now what do you think I heard it say?
CLUCK!
  CLUCK!
    CLUCK!

I went to visit a farm one day
And saw a duck across the way.
Now what do you think I heard it say?
QUACK!
QUACK!
QUACK!

I went to visit a farm one day
And saw a cow across the way.
Now what do you think I heard it say?
MOO!
MOO!
MOO!

I went to visit a farm one day
And saw *all* the animals across the way.
Now what do you think I heard them say?

OINK! BAA! CLUCK! QUACK! MOO-O-OO!

DINGLE-DANGLE SCARECROW

When all the cows were sleeping,
And the sun had gone to bed,
Up jumped the scarecrow,
And this is what he said:
"I'm a dingle-dangle scarecrow
With a flippy, floppy hat.
I can shake my hands like this,
I can shake my feet like that!"

When all the hens were roosting,
And the moon behind a cloud,
Up jumped the scarecrow,
And shouted very loud:
"I'M A DINGLE-DANGLE SCARECROW,
WITH A FLIPPY, FLOPPY HAT!
I CAN SHAKE MY ARMS LIKE THIS,
I CAN SHAKE MY LEGS LIKE THAT!"

M and G Russell-Smith

Horsie, horsie, don't you stop,
Just let your feet go clippety clop;
Your tail goes swish and the wheels go round —
Giddy-up, we're homeward bound.

Horsie, horsie, on your way,
We've done the journey many a day;
Your tail goes swish and the wheels go round —
Giddy-up, we're homeward bound.

PLOFFSKIN PLUFFSKIN PELICAN JEE!

THE PELICAN CHORUS

King and Queen of the Pelicans we;
No other birds so grand we see!
None but we have feet like fins!
With lovely leathery throats and chins!

Wing to wing we dance around,
Stamping our feet with a flumpy sound,
Opening our mouths as Pelicans ought,
And this is the song we nightly snort:

Ploffskin, Pluffskin, Pelican jee!
We think no birds so happy as we!
Plumpskin, Ploshkin, Pelican jill!
We think so then, and we thought so still!

Edward Lear (extract)

THE BIG BRASS BAND

Ten tom-toms
Timpany, too.
Ten tall tubas
And an old kazoo.

Ten trombones -
Give them a hand!
The sitting-standing-marching-running
Big Brass Band.

Glorious Mud

Mud! Mud! Glorious mud!
Nothing quite like it
For cooling the blood.
So follow me, follow,
Down to the hollow,
And there let us wallow
In glo-o-o-o-rious mud!

Michael Flanders

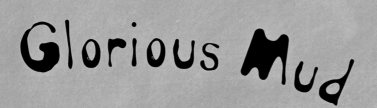

Pitter-patter Raindrops

I hear thunder.
I hear thunder.
Hark! Don't you?
Hark! Don't you?
Pitter-patter, raindrops,
Pitter-patter, raindrops.
I'm wet through,
So are you!

There was a young lady of Spain
Who couldn't go out in the rain
'Cause she'd lent her umbrella
To Queen Isabella
Who never returned it again.

One misty, moisty morning,
When cloudy was the weather,
I met a little old man
Clothed all in leather.

He bowed most politely,
And I began to grin.
How do you do? And how do you do?
And how do you do again?

Rain
on the green grass,
Rain
on the tree,
Rain
on the housetop –
But
not on me!

39

Wiggly Worms and Spindly Spiders

Slowly, slowly, very slowly
Creeps the garden snail,
Slowly, slowly, very slowly
Up the wooden rail.

Quickly, quickly, very quickly
Runs the little mouse,
Quickly, quickly, very quickly
Round about the house.

Salt, mustard, vinegar, cider,
How many legs has a great big spider?
Two, four, six, EIGHT!
Eight spindly legs on a great big spider.

Dandelion! dandelion!
Puff! puff! puff!
First you blow it gently
Then you blow it rough!
Wh-hhhh . . . uff!

Under a stone
Where the earth was firm,
I found a wiggly, wriggly worm;
"Good morning," I said.
"How are you today?"
But the wriggly worm
Just wriggled away!

41

SHARK

I swim with a grin up to greet you
See how my jaws open wide,
Why don't you come a bit closer?
Please, take a good look inside...

Giles Andreae

Oh No! Here We Go!

Oh, Jemima,
Look at your Uncle Jim!
He's down in the duck pond
Learning how to swim.
First he's on his
Left leg.
Then he's on his
Right.
Now he's on a bar of soap
Skidding out of
Sight!

One, two, three,
Mother caught a flea,
She put it in the teapot
And made a cup of tea.
Flea jumped out,
Mother gave a shout –
Father came running
With his shirt tails out!

44

Miss Polly had a dolly
Who was sick, sick, sick,
So she phoned for the doctor
To come quick, quick, quick.

The doctor came
With his bag and his hat,
And he knocked at the door
With a rat-a-tat-tat.

He looked at the dolly
And he shook his head.
Then he said, "Miss Polly,
Put her straight to bed."

He wrote on a paper
For a pill, pill, pill.
"That'll make her better
Yes, it will, will, will!"

There was an old man called Michael Finnegan,
He grew whiskers on his chinnegan,
Along came the wind and blew then in again,
Poor old Michael Finnegan –
BEGIN AGAIN!

Goldilocks and the Three Bears

When Goldilocks went to the house of the bears
Oh, what did her blue eyes see?
A bowl that was huge and a bowl that was small,
And a bowl that was tiny and that was all,
And she counted them - one, two, three.

When Goldilocks went to the house of the bears
Oh, what did her blue eyes see?
A chair that was huge and a chair that was small,
And a chair that was tiny and that was all,
And she counted them - one, two, three.

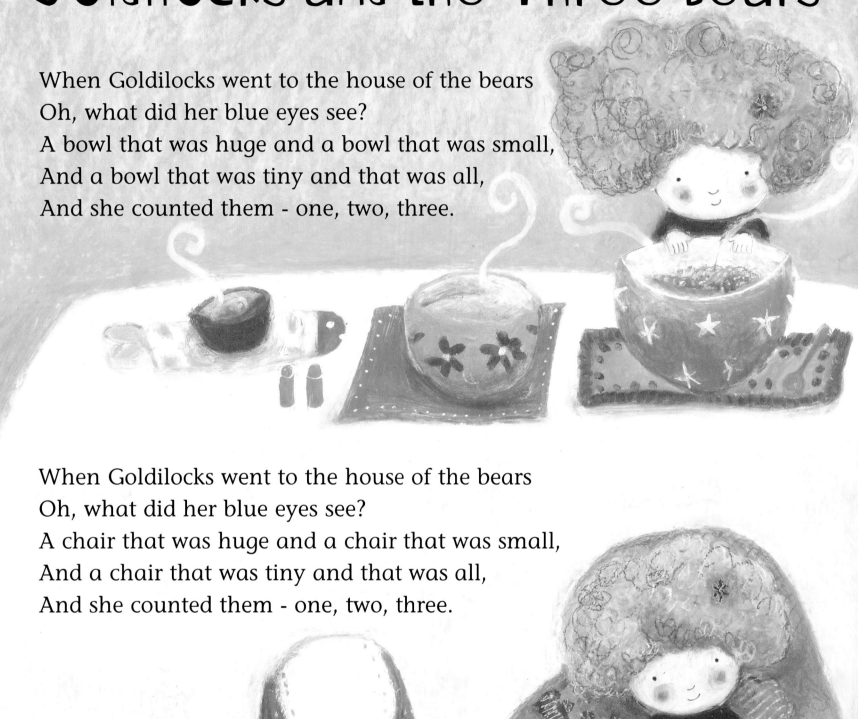

When Goldilocks went to the house of the bears
Oh, what did her blue eyes see?
A bed that was huge and a bed that was small,
And a bed that was tiny and that was all,
And she counted them - one, two, three.

When Goldilocks went to the house of the bears
Oh, what did her blue eyes see?
A bear that was huge and a bear that was small,
And a bear that was tiny and that was all,
And they growled at her - ROARR! ROARR! ROARR!

Carolyn Sherwin Bailey

Old Noah's Ark

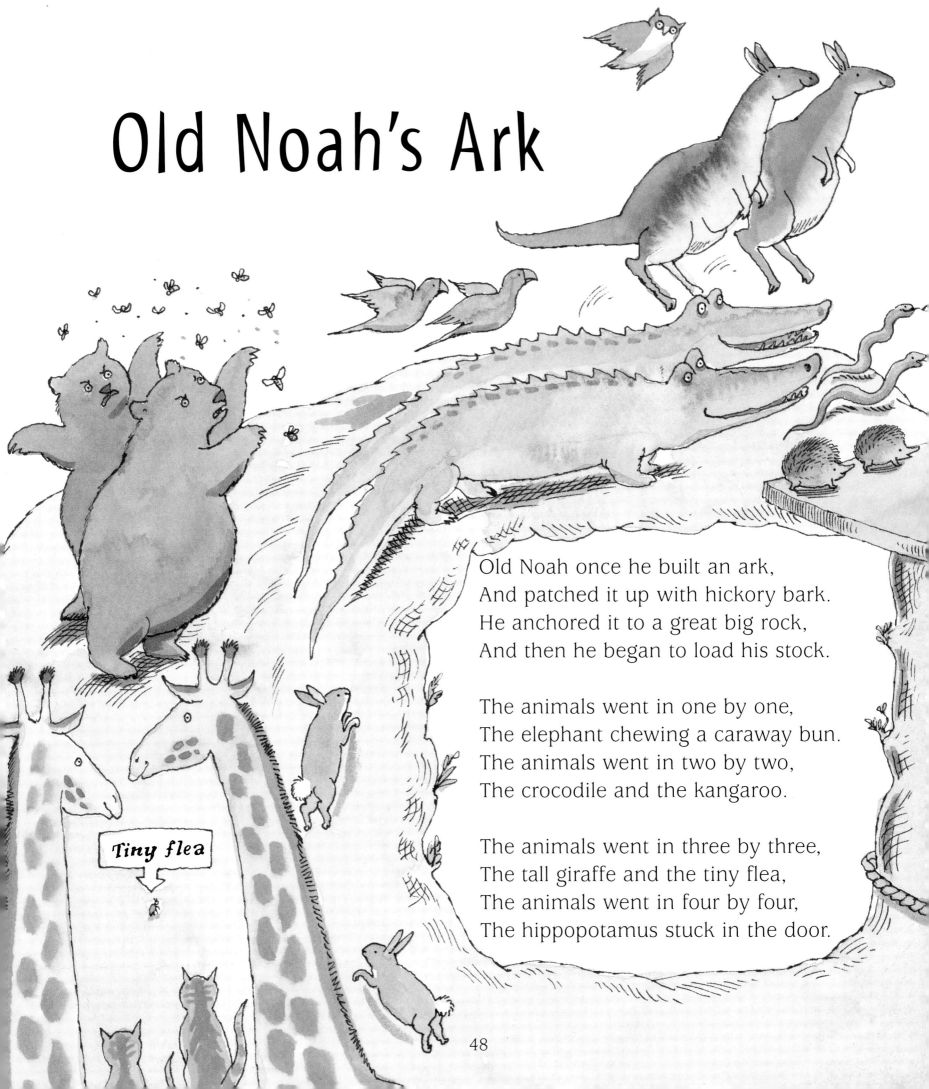

Tiny flea

Old Noah once he built an ark,
And patched it up with hickory bark.
He anchored it to a great big rock,
And then he began to load his stock.

The animals went in one by one,
The elephant chewing a caraway bun.
The animals went in two by two,
The crocodile and the kangaroo.

The animals went in three by three,
The tall giraffe and the tiny flea,
The animals went in four by four,
The hippopotamus stuck in the door.

The animals went in five by five,
The bees mistook the bear for a hive.
The animals went in six by six,
The monkey was up to his usual tricks.

The animals went in seven by seven,
Said the ant to the elephant, "Who are you shovin'?"
The animals went in eight by eight,
The tortoise was early, the rabbit was late.

The animals went in nine by nine,
They all formed fours and marched in a line.
The animals went in ten by ten,
If you want any more . . . you can read it again!

from The Tale of Custard the Dragon

Belinda lived in a little white house,
With a little black kitten and a little grey mouse,
And a little yellow dog and a little red wagon,
And a realio, trulio, little pet dragon.

Now the name of the little black kitten was Ink,
And the little grey mouse, she called her Blink,
And the little yellow dog was as sharp as Mustard,
But the dragon was a coward, and she called him Custard.

Custard the dragon had big sharp teeth,
And spikes on top of him and scales underneath,
Mouth like a fireplace, chimney for a nose,
And realio, trulio, daggers on his toes.

Ogden Nash

The Little Kittens

"Where are you going, my little kittens?"
"We are going to town to get us some mittens."
"What? Mittens for kittens?
Do kittens wear mittens?
Who ever saw little kittens with mittens?"

"Where are you going, my little cat?"
"I am going to town to get me a hat."
"What! A hat for a cat?
A cat get a hat!
Who ever saw a cat with a hat?"

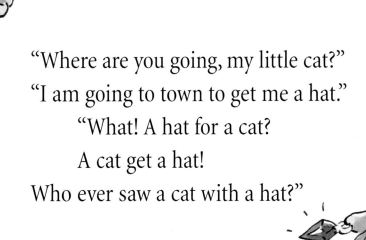

"Where are you going, my little pig?"
"I am going to town to get me a wig."
"What! A wig for a pig?
A pig in a wig!
Who ever saw a pig in a wig?"

Eliza Lee Follen

51

Giants
and Mice

Giant Jim, great giant Jim
Wears a hat without a brim,
Weighs a ton, can carry a house,
But trembles when he meets a mouse.

The Furry Home

If I were a mouse
And wanted a house,
I think I would choose
My new red shoes.

Furry edges,
Fur inside,
What a lovely
Place to hide!

I'd not travel,
I'd not roam –
Just sit in
My furry home.

J.M. Westrup

Frodge-Dobbulum

Did you ever see Giant Frodge-dobbulum,
With his double great-toe and his double great-thumb?

Did you ever hear Giant Frodge-dobbulum
Saying *Fa-Fe-Fi* and *fo-faw-fum*?

He shakes the earth as he walks along,
As deep as the sea, as far as Hong Kong!

He is a giant and no mistake,
With teeth like the prongs of a garden rake.

W.B. Rands (extract)

Mice

I think mice
Are rather nice.

Their tails are long,
Their faces small,
They haven't any
Chins at all.
Their ears are pink,
Their teeth are white,
They run about
The house at night.
They nibble things
They shouldn't touch
And no one seems
To like them much.

But *I* think mice
Are nice.

Rose Fyleman

On the Ning Nang Nong

On the Ning Nang Nong
Where the Cows go Bong!
And the Monkeys all say Boo!
There's a Nong Nang Ning
Where the trees go Ping!
And the teapots Jibber Jabber Joo.
On the Nong Ning Nang
All the mice go Clang!
And you can't catch 'em when they do!
So it's Ning Nang Nong!
Cows go Bong!
Nong Nang Ning!
Trees go Ping!
Nong Ning Nang!
The mice go Clang!
What a noisy place to belong,
Is the Ning Nang Ning Nang Nong!

Spike Milligan

Swan swam over the sea,
Swim, swan, swim!
Swan swam back again.
Well swum, swan!

Alfie Dean
Was rather mean;
He jumped on
Lucy's juicy
Jelly Bean.

"I guess," said Lucy,
"Alfie's a goosey
To jump on
My one juicy
Jelly Bean."

The Firemen

Clang! Clang! Clang!
Says the red fire bell –
'There's a big fire blazing
At the Grand Hotel!'

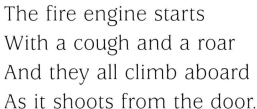

The firemen shout
As they tumble out of bed
And slide down the pole
To the fire engine shed.

The fire engine starts
With a cough and a roar
And they all climb aboard
As it shoots from the door.

Whee! Whee! Whee!
You can hear the cry
Of the siren shrieking
As they hurtle by.

At the Grand Hotel
There is smoke and steam.
Flames at the windows
And people who scream.

The biggest fireman
Carries down
A fat old lady
In her dressing gown.

When the fire is finished
The firemen go
Back through the same streets
Driving slow.

Home at the station
The firemen stay
And polish up the nozzles
For the next fire day.

James K. Baxter

Cows

The friendly cow all red and white,
I love with all my heart:
She gives me cream, with all her might,
To eat with apple tart.

R.L. Stevenson (extract)

Sometimes I moo while I'm chewing
I hope you don't think that it's rude,
But mooing and chewing
Are what I like doing,
Do you moo when you chew your food?

Giles Andreae

moo
chew
moo

Favourite Food

Honey Bear

There was a big bear
Who lived in a cave;
His greatest love
   Was honey.

He had twopence a week
Which he never could save,
So he never had
   Any money.

I bought him a money box,
Red and round,
In which to put
   His money.

He saved and saved
Till he got a pound,
Then spent it all
   On honey.

Elizabeth Lang

The cuckoo calls, *coo, coo, coo,*
Don't touch the mangoes any of you,
For I am the mango queen you see,
Eating mangoes is for me.

Banana Man

I'm a banana man
not a superman
or a batman
or a spiderman
No, man
Banana in the morning
Banana in the evening
Banana before I go to bed
at night – that's right
that's how much I love
the banana bite

Grace Nichols (extract)

If I were Teeny Tiny

If I were teeny tiny
If I were teeny tiny
A mouse could be my pony
And we'd gallop very hard.

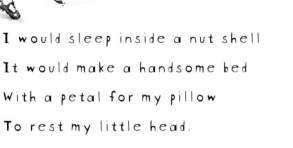

I would sleep inside a nut shell
It would make a handsome bed
With a petal for my pillow
To rest my little head.

If I were tiny teeny
If I were tiny teeny
I would swim when it was rainy
In a puddle in the yard.

I'd make dresses out of grasses
I'd weave slippers out of rushes
And instead of plates and glasses
I'd use leaves from off the bushes.

Oh the things that I would do
Are many many many
If I were teeny tiny
If I were teeny tiny.

Beatrice Schenk de Regniers

62

Ladybird, ladybird, fly from my hand,
Tell me where, tell me where my true love stands –
Up-hill or down-hill, or by the sea-sand,
Ladybird, ladybird, fly from my hand.

Pinkety,

  pinkety,

    thumb to thumb,

Wish a wish and it's sure to come.

From The Dream Fairy

A little fairy comes at night,
Her eyes are blue, her hair is brown,
With silver spots upon her wings,
And from the moon she flutters down.

She has a little silver wand,
And when a good child goes to bed
She waves her wand from right to left
And makes a circle round her head.

Thomas Hood

One for Sorrow, Two for Joy...

I saw seven magpies in a tree:

One for sorrow,

Two for joy,

Three for a girl,

Four for a boy,

Five for silver,

Six for gold,

Seven for a secret never to be told.

Here is the beehive.
Where are the bees?
Hidden away where nobody sees,
Here they come creeping, out of the hive,
One, two, three, four, five.

z z z z z z z z z z ...

Five little owls in an old elm-tree,
Fluffy and puffy as owls could be,
Blinking and winking with big round eyes
At the big round moon that hung in the skies:
As I passed beneath, I could hear one say,
"There'll be mouse for supper, there will, today!"
Then all of them hooted "*Tu-whit, Tu-whoo!*
Yes, mouse for supper, *Hoo-hoo, Hoo-hoo!*"

Chook-chook, chook-chook-chook!
Good morning, Mrs Hen.
How many chickens have you got?
Madam, I've got ten.
Four of them are yellow,
And four of them are brown,
And two of them are speckled red,
The nicest in the town.

Five Little Monkeys

Five little monkeys
Walked by the shore.
One sailed off –
So that left four.

Four little monkeys
Climbed up a tree.
One fell down –
So that left three.

Three little monkeys
Found some sticky glue.
One got stuck in it –
So that left two.

Two little monkeys
Found a currant bun.
One ran off with it –
So that left one.

One little monkey
Worked hard all afternoon.
He built himself a space-ship –
And flew off to the moon.

Song of the Train

Clickety-clack,

Wheels on the track,

This is the way

They begin the attack:

Click-ety-clack,

Click-ety-clack,

Click-ety, *clack-ety*,

Click-ety

Clack.

Clickety-clack,

Over the crack,

Faster and faster

The song of the track:

Clickety-clack,

Clickety-clack,

Clickety, clackety,

Clackety

Clack.

Riding in front,

Riding in back,

Everyone hears,

The song of the track:

Clickety-clack,

Clickety-clack,

Clickety, *clickety*,

Clackety

Clack.

David McCord

Flying-man! Flying-man!
Up in the sky,
Where are you going to
Flying so high?

Over the mountains,
Over the sea.
Flying-man! Flying-man!
Please take me!

Ahoy There!

One-eyed Jack, the pirate chief,
Was a terrible, fearsome ocean thief.
He wore a peg
Upon one leg;
He wore a hook –
And a dirty look!
One-eyed Jack, the pirate chief –
A terrible, fearsome ocean thief!

Once there was a Whale   Whaly Scaly Shaly   Tumbly-taily   Mighty Whale!

Edward Lear

Sail Away Song

Ahoy, me jolly hearties,
we're going on a trip,
beyond the bay and far away
in our jolly ship.

One sailor has a needle
for patching up the sail.
One has got a telescope –
Look! There goes a whale!

One is knitting rigging.
One is sipping tea.
One is swinging from
   the yardarm.
There she goes –
   wheeeeee!

One is knocking nails in
(the one whose scarf is red).
One is trying to catch a fish
with a worm and thread.

The captain's giving orders,
ooh arh! in sailor talk.
"Aye-aye," says his parrot.
"Squawk, squawk, squawk!"

Tony Mitton

Up in Cities, Down on Farms

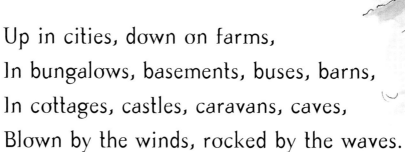

Up in cities, down on farms,
In bungalows, basements, buses, barns,
In cottages, castles, caravans, caves,
Blown by the winds, rocked by the waves.

In busy harbours, perched on sticks,
In igloos of ice and towers of bricks,
On mountains, islands, snow and sand,
Families together in every land.

Laurence and Catherine Anholt

72

You, North must go,
To a hut of snow;
You, South in a trice,
To an island of spice;

You, East fly high,
On a carpet in the sky;
You, West heave ho,
To the land of the buffalo;

North, South, East, West,
Home is the place
I like the best!

Secret Places

The Cupboard

I know a little cupboard,
With a teeny tiny key,
And there's a jar of Lollipops
    For me, me, me.

It has a little shelf, my dear,
As dark as dark can be,
And there's a dish of Banbury cakes
    For me, me, me.

I have a small fat grandmamma,
With a very slippery knee,
And she's Keeper of the Cupboard,
    With the key, key, key.

And when I'm very good, my dear,
As good as good can be,
There's Banbury Cakes and Lollipops
    For me, me, me.

Walter de la Mare

Grandad's Shed

Grandad's shed is a secret place.
I love to go in there,
And when I say, "Please, Grandad, please!"
He finds the key, unlocks the door,
And we step inside.

There's watering cans and a lawnmower,
Forks and flowerpots too.
A spade, a rake, a trowel,
Sharp saws for cutting through.

There's sticks and bags and paint tins,
Seed packets, balls of string,
A stepladder, a box of tools
All sorts of curious things.

When we've finished looking,
And closed the door and turned the key,
What does my Grandad do?

He swings me high, then sits me down,
Snug in his green wheelbarrow.
"Hold tight!" he says,
And off we go,
The two of us together.

Margaret Mayo

What Will the Weather be Like Today?

Just at the moment
when night becomes day,
when the stars in the sky
begin fading away,
you can hear all the birds
and the animals say,
"What will the weather
be like today?"

Will it be windy?
Will it be warm?
Will there be snow?
Or a frost?
Or a storm?

"Be dry," says the lizard,
"and *I* won't complain."
The frog in the bog says,
"Perhaps it will rain."

The white cockatoo
likes it steamy and hot.
The mole doesn't know
if it's raining or not.
"Whatever the weather,
I work," says the bee.
"Wet," says the duck,
"is the weather for me."
"Weather? What's that?"
say the fish in the sea.

The world has awoken.
The day has begun,
and somewhere it's cloudy,
and somewhere there's sun,
and somewhere the sun
and the rain meet to play,
and paint a bright rainbow
to dress up the day!

How is the weather
where *you* are today?
Paul Rogers

Hey-ho for Halloween!

Double, double,
Toil and trouble;
Fire – burn
And cauldron – bubble.

William Shakespeare

'Witch, witch, where do you fly?'
'Under the clouds and over the sky.'

'Witch, witch, what do you eat?'
'Little black apples from Hurricane Street.'

'Witch, witch, what do you drink?'
'Vinegar, blacking and good red ink.'

'Witch, witch, where do you sleep?'
'Up in the clouds where the pillows are cheap.'

Rose Fyleman

Late on a dark and stormy night
Three witches stirred with all their might.
Two little ghosts said, "How d'ye do?"
The wizard went tiptoe, tiptoe . . .
    BOOOOOOO!

B was a bat
Who slept all the day
And fluttered about,
When the sun went away.
        b!
Brown little bat!

Edward Lear

Hey-ho for Halloween,
All the witches to be seen,
Some black and some green,
Hey-ho for Halloween!

Wibble Wobble

Jelly on the plate,
Jelly on the plate,
Wibble-wobble, wibble-wobble,
Jelly on the plate.

Sausages in the pan,
Sausages in the pan,
Turn them over, turn them over,
Sausages in the pan.

Ghostie in the house,
Ghostie in the house,
Turn him out, turn him out,
Ghostie in the house.

Hot cross buns!
Hot cross buns!
One a penny, two a penny,
Hot cross buns!

Give them to your daughters,
Give them to your sons:
One a penny, two a penny,
Hot cross buns!

The Pancake

Mix a pancake,
Stir a pancake,
Pop it in the pan.

Fry the pancake,
Toss the pancake –
Catch it if you can.

Christina Rossetti

Ladies and gentlemen,
Come to supper –
There's hot baked beans
And very good butter.

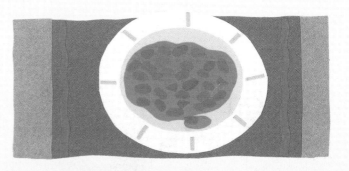

CHRISTMAS PUDDING

Into the basin put the plums,
Stir-about, stir-about, stir-about!

Next the good white flour comes,
Stir-about, stir-about, stir-about!

Sugar and peel and eggs and spice,
Stir-about, stir-about, stir-about!

Mix them and fix them and cook them twice,
Stir-about, stir-about, stir-about!

When Santa got stuck up the chimney,
He began to shout:
"You girls and boys won't get any toys
If you don't pull me out!
My beard is black,
    There's soot in my sack,
        My nose is tickling too."
        When Santa got stuck up the chimney,
            ATCHOO! ATCHOO! ATCHOO!

The
More
it
Snows

The more it
SNOWS–tiddely-pom,
The more it
GOES–tiddely-pom
The more it
GOES–tiddely-pom
On
Snowing.

And nobody
KNOWS–tiddely-pom,
How cold my
TOES–tiddely-pom
How cold my
TOES–tiddely-pom
Are
Growing.

A.A. Milne

The north wind doth blow
And we shall have snow,
And what will the robin do then,
  Poor thing?
He'll sit in a barn,
And keep himself warm,
And hide his head under his wing,
  Poor thing!

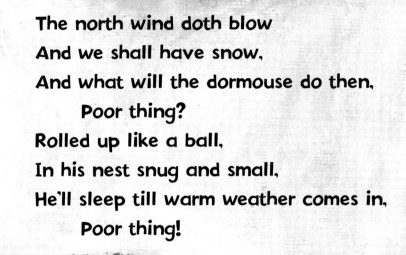

The north wind doth blow
And we shall have snow,
And what will the dormouse do then,
    Poor thing?
Rolled up like a ball,
In his nest snug and small,
He'll sleep till warm weather comes in,
    Poor thing!

Juniper, Juniper,
Green in the snow;
Sweetly you smell,
And prickly you grow.

Juniper, Juniper,
Blue in the fall:
Give me some berries,
Prickles and all.

Kings Came Riding

Kings came riding,
   One, two and three,
Over the desert
   And over the sea.

One in a ship
   With a silver mast;
The fishermen wondered
   As he went past.

One on a horse
   With a saddle of gold;
The children came running
   To behold.

One came walking,
   Over the sand,
With a casket of treasure
   Held in his hand.

All the people
   Said 'where go they?'
But the kings went foward
   All through the day.

Night came on
   And those kings went by;
They shone like the gleaming
   Stars in the sky.

Charles Williams

Star light, star bright,
First star I see tonight,
I wish I may, I wish I might,
Have the wish I wish tonight.

Sing A Lullaby

The White Seal

Oh! hush thee, my baby, the night is behind us,
And black are the waters that sparkled so green.
The moon o'er the combers, looks downward to find us
At rest in the hollows that rustle between.

Where billow meets billow, there soft be thy pillow;
Ah, weary wee flipperling, curl at thy ease!
The storm shall not wake thee, nor shark overtake thee,
Asleep in the arms of the slow-swinging seas.

Rudyard Kipling

The Tree Bear

Listen to the tree bear
Crying in the night
Crying for his mammy
In the pale moonlight.

What will his mammy do
When she hears him cry?
She'll tuck him in a cocoa pod
And sing a lullaby.

Peggy Appiah

Hush Little Baby

Hush little baby, don't say a word,
Mama's going to buy you *a mockingbird*.

And if that mockingbird won't sing,
Mama's going to buy you *a diamond ring*.

And if that diamond ring turns to brass,
Mama's going to buy you *a looking-glass*.

If that looking-glass gets broke,
Mama's going to buy you *a billy-goat*.

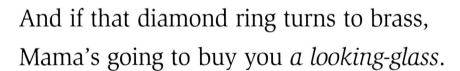

And if that billy-goat won't pull,
Mama's going to buy you *a cart and bull*.

And if that cart and bull turn over,
Mama's going to buy you *a dog named Rover*.

And if that dog named Rover won't bark,
Mama's going to buy you *a horse and cart*.

And if that horse and cart fall down,
You'll still be the sweetest little baby in town.

Good Night

Someone

Someone came knocking
   At my wee, small door;
Someone came knocking,
   I'm sure – sure – sure;
I listened, I opened,
   I looked to left and right,
But nought there was a-stirring
   In the still dark night;
Only the busy beetle
   Tap-tapping in the wall,
Only from the forest
   The screech-owl's call,
Only the cricket whistling
   While the dewdrops fall,
So I know not who came knocking,
   At all, at all, at all.

Walter de la Mare

How many miles to Babylon?
Three score and ten.

Can I get there by candle-light?
Yes, and back again.

Then open the gates without more ado,
And let the king and his men pass through.

Here's a body – there's a bed!
There's a pillow – here's a head!
There's a curtain – here's a light!
There's a puff – and so good night!

Thomas Hood

Index

Acknowledgements

'Hopaloo Kangaroo' from WE ANIMALS WOULD LIKE A WORD WITH YOU published by Bodley Head 1996, reprinted by kind permission of John Agard c/o Caroline Sheldon Literary Agency; 'Shark' by Giles Andreae reproduced by permission of The Peters Fraser and Dunlop Group Limited on behalf of © Purple Enterprises Ltd; 'Cow' by Giles Andreae reproduced by permission of The Peters Fraser and Dunlop Group Limited on behalf of © Purple Enterprises Ltd; 'Up in Cities, Down on Farms' by Laurence and Catherine Anholt from BIG BOOK OF FAMILIES © 1998 Laurence and Catherine Anholt, reproduced by permission of the publisher Walker Books Ltd., London; 'Witch, Witch, Where do You Fly?' and 'Wanted' Reprinted with permission from The Society of Authors as the Literary Representative of the Estate of Rose Fyleman; 'Engineers' by Jimmy Garthwaite copyright 1929 by HarperCollins publishers, renewed © 1957 by Mirle Garthwaite, used by permission of HarperCollins publishers; 'The White Seal' by Rudyard Kipling reproduced by permission of A.P. Watt Ltd on behalf of The National Trust for places of Historic Interest or Natural Beauty; 'Honey Bear' © Elizabeth Lang reprinted with permission of HarperCollins publishers Ltd; 'The Cupboard' and 'Someone' reprinted with permission of The Literary Trustees of Walter de la Mare and The Society of Authors as their representative; 'Alfie Dean' Anonymous, Verse 2 ©; Maragaret Mayo 'Puff!' Traditional, adapted by Margaret Mayo; 'Grandad's Shed' © Margaret Mayo; 'On the Ning Nang Nong' © Spike Milligan; 'The More It Snows' from THE HUMS OF POOH © A.A. Milne Copyright under the Berne Convention, published by Mammoth, an imprint of Egmont Children's Books Ltd, London, and used with permission; Sail Away Song © Tony Mitton 2001, 'Banana Man' reproduced with permission of Curtis Brown Ltd, London, on behalf of Grace Nichols. Copyright Grace Nichols 1988; 'You, North Must Go' Anonymous, verses 2 and 3 © Juliet Nolan; 'The Frog on the Log' by Ilo Orleans © Karen S. Solomon. From THE ZOO THAT GREW by Ilo Orleans; 'The Yak' text copyright © Jack Prelutsky used by permission of HarperCollins Publishers; 'The Princess Priscilla' © E.V. Rieu; 'What Will the Weather Be Like Today?' Text copyright Paul Rogers, first published by Orchard Books 1989; 'Humpty Dumpty' Reprinted by permission of The Peters Fraser and Dunlop Group Ltd on behalf of Michael Rosen. © Michael Rosen; 'Dingle Dangle Scarecrow' Music by Geoffrey Russell-Smith, words by Mollie Russell-Smith. Worldwide print rights controlled by Warner Bros Publications Inc/IMP Ltd. Lyrics reproduced by permission of IMP Ltd. All rights reserved; 'Kings Came Riding' by Charles Williams from MODERN VOICES FOR LITTLE CHILDREN, reproduced with permission from David Higham Associates.